THE MAGICAL TEDDY BEAR

AUTHOR: SUSAN LACEY
ILLUSTRATOR: LOUISE RABEY
DESIGNER: ADRIAN LACEY

COPYRIGHT

This book is published by
Grosvenor House Publishing Ltd
Link House
140 The Broadway, Tolworth, Surrey, KT6 7HT.
www.grosvenorhousepublishing.co.uk

A CIP record for this book
is available from the British Library

ISBN 978-1-78623-453-7

DEDICATIONS

To You, For Buying This Magical Book

A MAGICAL TEDDY BEAR FOREWORD BY ACTRESS VERONICA TAYLOR

BEST KNOWN AS THE VOICE OF THE LEAD CHARACTER, ASH KETCHUM IN THE HIT ANIME SERIES "Pokémon"

In "The Magical Teddy Bear", Susan Lacey has captured the transformative power of imagination and the strength we get from helping others. You don't have to be a superhero to make a difference... but wearing a cape is always a good idea!

The whimsical illustrations of Louise Rabey, coupled with the design skills of Susan's Son, Adrian Lacey, allow us to easily escape into and spend time in this wonderful world.

This is a lovely bedtime story which will inspire many sweet dreams.

Veronica Taylor

The Magical Teddy Bear

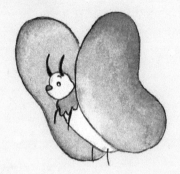

Author: Susan Lacey
Illustrator: Louise Rabey
Designer: Adrian Lacey

A small and scruffy brown teddy bear
Lay silently on the bedroom floor.
It was terribly old and tatty,
With a crooked ear and a scraggly paw.

The big round smiling moon
Shone with a much brighter glow,
As it dropped a sparkling beam
Onto the bear below.

Petals and glittering stardust
Fell like snow all around,
Where the dilapidated teddy bear
Lay in silence on the ground.

3

The bear's dull fur turned a golden colour
And its two dark eyes became so bright,
As it sat in the flaring beams
Of the dazzling moonlight.

The transformed teddy bear
Stayed for a while in the gleaming glow
And then it started to move
Ever so... ever so... slow...

And it was bathed in light from its head to each furry toe.

The amazing teddy bear then came alive
And seemed to know just what to do,
As it twirled and swirled around,
Looking just like it was brand new.

"I am truly magical now,
That is for sure,"
The bear said as it stamped its two furry feet
On the bedroom floor.

The wonderful teddy bear
Had spots and stars before its big dark eyes,
As he felt his strong new velvety body
Slowly begin to rise.

He felt like a giant deep within,
As he grew impressive wings on either side.
He wore a tea cosy and a red velvet cloak,
With so much joy and pride.

9

He flew right out of his cosy home,
Just like a hero through the satin sky,
As the cloud, the breeze, the moon and the stars sang
A most haunting lullaby.

"Teddy bears are stuffed toys
And quite simply do not fly"
Said a passing nosey and inquisitive
Gigantic butterfly.

"I do, because I was ordinary,
But now, I am quite magical, you see
And there is no other bear in the world,
That is quite as strong and brave as me."

"I am going right now
To save the whole wide world,
With my supersonic powers
And my red velvet cloak unfurled."

He then flew off like the speed of light,
Into the darkness, on this magical night.

Then the truly Magical Teddy Bear whizzed down
And helped a massive lion in a zoo,
That had caught its head between the bars
And had turned a shade of blue!

Saying "Roar Roar, Thank you,
You have a kind heart that is good and true."

15

The next thing he did was to help a silly chicken
Cross the road to the other side,
As it had just laid an unusual egg,
That was both long and wide!

The chicken said "Cluck Cluck, Thank you,
You have a kind heart that is good and true."

He then fought an evil scaly dragon,
That was standing on top of a castle wall
And rescued a cute baby dinosaur,
That was very timid, shy and small...

The scared little thing just nodded its head
And said nothing much at all.

Then he helped an old pink pig,
That had lost all of his front teeth.
They were lying in between his enormous trotters,
That were stood on the pathway that laid beneath!

"Oink Oink, Thank you" he said.
Before he hobbled back home to his warm pigsty bed.

21

The super hero bear went across the universe,
Helping animals and people that were in distress
And he aided an old lady, wearing big round glasses,
With an angry crab creeping up the side of her dress!

He brushed it off with one swish and swipe of his wing,
So that she did not even notice one single thing.

Then the Magical Teddy Bear aided a magnificent owl,
That had a badly broken wing.
He touched it with his gentle paw to make it better,
Until the owl began to sing.

"To-Wit To-Woo, Thank you,
You have a kind heart that is good and true."

A kind elephant came trudging along,
And gave the Magical Teddy Bear a ride on
his strong back of velvety grey.

"This is a special treat just for you,
As you have helped many other needy folks
along the way."

The bear said "Thank you, but I must be going,
While the black of night is showing."

27

The Magical Teddy Bear came to sit and rest
Upon a chimney pot that was very high.
He thought about what he had done that night,
As he looked towards the sky.

29

But... then... he suddenly felt his supersonic energy and power,
Slowly beginning to wane,
So that he had to make his humble way,
Back to his cosy home once again.

He took off his tea cosy hat and cloak,
That was a pure velvety red,
Just as the magnificent butterfly came in
And landed on the top of his head!

Then the golden Magical Teddy Bear,
Became brown and scruffy once more,
As it slowly and silently fell backwards,
Onto the carpeted floor.

So...the cloud, the breeze, the moon and the stars,
Gave a gentle and knowing kind of sigh,
As they all sang together in harmony...
A most haunting lullaby.

FROM THE AUTHOR

So here is Children's book No 4,
The start of yet another series.
My first three books were the
Jolly Quickly Trilogy. This is where I
wish to thank all those who have made
this fantastic picture story book possible.

First to my tremendous son for spending hours and hours
designing and setting out the text.

To Veronica Taylor for her immensely beautiful Foreword that
says it all about the book. Other stories are waiting in the wings
to come out in this new series.

Last, but certainly not least, to Louise Rabey for her immaculate
eye catching illustrations that complement my work so very well.

With Love
SUSAN

About the Author

I am Susan Lacey from the Chiltern Hills.

I am first and foremost a writer of children's story books but also write comedy and reflective poetry, compose songs, plays and musicals.

I am also well known for performing locally my comedy poetry amongst other things.

I gain my inspiration from the world around me and from the things people say.

My intention is always to bring happiness and enjoyment to the reader or listener of my work.

SUSAN

A WORD FROM THE DESIGNER

Working on this book in my numerous capacities, has been an honour & a pleasure to help convert my mum's writing into the finished article you can now read.

I hope reading this absolutely magically amazing story brings you enjoyment.
Reading is so important, whether read to a child to aid in a smooth imaginative dream filled night's sleep, to being used as an educational tool.
Books are a valuable, inexpensive, yet colourful way to expand our minds & of course fall into a magical fantasy world.
I wish to express huge thanks to Louise Rabey, who has shown such talent in bringing my design ideas alive, also to the lovely Veronica Taylor, a talented actress, known for being the voice of Ash Ketchum from Pokémon, who kindly agreed to support us with a most fabulous foreword in this book.

Finally a HUGE, HUGE, MEGA THANKS To EVERYONE involved in any way with this book, ESPECIALLY YOU for supporting this book.
Please do look for Susan's other children's books, they are truly magical.
Best Magical Wishes, Adrian :-)

Veronica Taylor with me at ComicCon

CONTACT

Email The Author:
TheMagicalTeddyBear@gmail.com

Contact The Illustrator:
louiserabeyart@gmail.com
www.louise-rabey-art.com

Follow The Designer On Twitter:
@al4wfc

Other Works of Mine

Childrens Books
The Jolly Quickly The Jumping Bean Trilogy
Written By Susan Lacey – Illustrated By Nicolas Milano – Design By Adrian Lacey
Jolly Quickly The Jumping Bean (His First Jumping Day)
Jolly Quickly The Jumping Bean Rockets Into Space
(Includes A Foreword From Doctor Who Actress – Katy Manning)
Jolly Quickly The Jumping Bean Goes Under The Sea
(Includes A Foreword From Doctor Who Actress – Katy Manning)

Adult Comedy & Reflective Poetry Book
At The Drop Of A Hat
Written By Susan Lacey – Design/Photography By Adrian Lacey

MUSIC
One Life - Fully Written & Composed By Susan Lacey (Performed By Kirsta Johnston)
On The Back Of A Tear – Fully Written & Composed By Susan Lacey (Performed By Daisy Soul)

To Keep Posted Of Future Books & Music Related Releases Email
TheMagicalTeddyBear@gmail.com
With the email title- Keep Me Informed
Thank You For Your Support
The Magical Teddy Bear

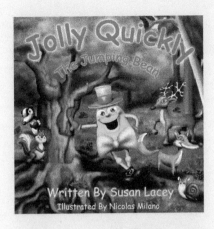

CPSIA information can be obtained
at www.ICGtesting.com
Printed in the USA
BVHW021703170419
545819BV00023B/316/P

9 781786 234537